For my little family –
every day, now and always, all my love. XO!
– N B

With love to Louise and Eloise
– J L

LITTLE TIGER PRESS
1 The Coda Centre, 189 Munster Road,
London SW6 6AW

First published in Great Britain 2016
Text copyright © Nicky Benson 2016
Illustrations copyright © Jonny Lambert 2016

A CIP catalogue record for this book is available from
the British Library
· ISBN 978-1-84869-211-4

Printed in China · LTP/1800/1244/0915

2 4 6 8 10 9 7 5 3 1

I love you
you
more
and more

Nicky Benson

Jonny Lambert

LITTLE TIGER PRESS
London

You are my everything,
I love you high and low.

I love you more than flowers
love to blossom, bloom and grow.

I love you more than trees love to change with every season.

I love you more than anything,

I cannot name just one reason.

I love you more than waterfalls
love to splash on me and you.

I love you more than fish
love to swim in rivers blue.

I love you more than mountains
love the clouds breezing by.

I love you more than stars
love to sparkle in the sky.

You are beautiful in all you do,
and in all the words you say . . .

I love you, baby, more and more with every precious day.